CAPTURED
in Canton

by
Phil Hardwick

QUAIL RIDGE PRESS
Brandon, Mississippi

Other books in Phil Hardwick's Mississippi Mysteries Series:

Found in Flora

Justice in Jackson

Newcomer in New Albany

Vengeance in Vicksburg

Collision in Columbia

Conspiracy in Corinth

To be included on the Mississippi Mysteries mailing list, please send your name and complete mailing address to:

QUAIL RIDGE PRESS
P. O. Box 123 • Brandon, MS 39043
1-800-343-1583

DEDICATION

This one is for Clay,
who adds immense joy to my life.

ACKNOWLEDGMENTS

The author is deeply appreciative of the assistance and information received from the citizens of Canton, who shared their stories, homes, and businesses. A special note of thanks to Deborah, Nina and Chip. I owe much gratitude to the Canton Chamber of Commerce, who made this project come to life. The community is fortunate to have such a group of dedicated people.

I hope that all who read this book will do what I have done—discover Canton.

PROLOGUE

The small single-engine, four-seat airplane sliced through the October night sky at eight-thousand feet, enroute to the Madison Airport from Destin, Florida. Thirty-five miles southeast of Jackson, Mississippi, the Memphis Center handed off the aircraft to Jackson Approach Control. The time was ten-thirteen p.m.

9859Lima: Jackson Approach, this is niner-eight-five-niner Lima. I'm with you at five thousand.

Control: Roger, niner-eight-five-niner Lima. Radar contact thirty-five miles southeast of Jackson. Descend and maintain three thousand. Expect visual approach to Madison Airport. Jackson Altimeter two-niner-niner-two.

9859Lima: Jackson Approach, niner-eight-five-niner Lima leaving five thousand for three-thousand.

Control: Niner-eight-five-niner Lima, Madison Airport twelve o'clock, one-zero miles. Report the airport in sight.

9859Lima: Jackson Approach, niner-eight-five-niner Lima. Madison Airport in sight.

Control: Roger, niner-eight-five-niner Lima. Cleared for visual approach to Madison Airport.

9859Lima: Jackson Approach, niner-eight-five-niner Lima. At this time cancel IFR flight plan for visual approach.

Control: Roger, niner-eight-five-niner Lima. Squawk

twelve-zero-zero. Radar service terminated. Frequency change approved.

9859Lima: Mayday! Mayday!

The radar screen flashed 7700, the international distress signal.

Chapter 1

It was in midmorning on the first Friday in October when I got the call from David Edelman, vice president of Loss Prevention of a large insurance company headquartered in Cambridge, Massachusetts. He sounded as urgent as any man whose company stood to pay out five million dollars.

"Jack, we need to retain your services again," he said in his Boston brogue. "Did you read about that small plane that went down in the Barnett Reservoir, night before last?"

"Yes, I did," I replied. "I have the newspaper article right here in front of me."

"Good," he said. "Find out as much as you can about that plane crash. The pilot took out a five million dollar policy with us just over a month ago. I'll fax you a copy of the application, and a copy of our file on him. It's one of those cases that doesn't pass the nose test, as we say in my business."

"In other words, it stinks," I said.

"Exactly right," he said. "Is the same fee structure we used in our last case satisfactory?"

"It is," I said, recalling that nine months ago I had documented and disproved a series of fraudulent disability claims. It saved the company hundreds of thousands of dollars, and I had been paid well for my services.

"Good. So how is Jack Boulder, Mississippi's best private investigator, these days?"

"Couldn't be better," I said.

"I'm glad to hear that. The information is on its way. We look forward to your report as soon as possible."

We said our goodbyes, and instantly the fax machine in my bedroom office started whirring. I live in a three-bedroom condominium overlooking Smith Park in downtown Jackson, Mississippi, and I operate my private investigator service from bedroom number three, the one downstairs with no windows. Equipped with state-of-the-art computer and electronic equipment, I don't need a rent-gobbling office or a secretary. I also do not need to work unless I want to, because of my retirement check that arrives on the fifth of each month from the City of St. Louis, where I spent twenty years on the police department—most of them in the homicide bureau. For a single guy approaching his mid-forties, it is not a bad way to make a living.

A few minutes later, twelve pages of documents made their telecommute from Boston to Jackson. I scanned them quickly and immediately saw the reason for the insurance company's concern. The applicant was a thirty-nine-year-old married white male from Destin, Florida, by the name of Larry Watson. His occupation was listed as trade show dealer, and although he had paid an astronomical premium for the policy, his credit report showed that he had several late-pay accounts and two judgments in the past five years. The beneficiary was listed as his wife. Six years ago, he had been arrested in Memphis on a charge of false pretenses, but the charges had been dropped.

I picked up my copy of the *Clarion-Ledger* newspaper and read the account of the plane crash. It reported that at approximately ten-thirty this past Tuesday evening, a four-passenger, single engine plane went down in the Barnett Reservoir. Divers found the plane, which was intact and resting upside down in the water. It was registered to the Avion Flying Service in Destin, Florida, and had been rented Tuesday. The name of the pilot was being withheld at this time. As of late Thursday afternoon, the body of the pilot had not been recovered. The plane was expected to be lifted out of the water Friday morning.

An hour later I was sitting across from the Chief of Law Enforcement of the Pearl River Water Supply District, in whose jurisdiction the plane had crashed. "The District," as it is called, was formed to own and operate the Barnett Reservoir, which was created in the mid-sixties when the Pearl River was dammed just north of Jackson. That ownership involves everything from real estate development, to law enforcement, to providing a safe supply of drinking water. Throw in recreation, and it is one large operation—given the fact that the reservoir has a shoreline of over one hundred miles.

Being Chief of Law Enforcement of an operation that size is equivalent to being sheriff of a large county or chief of police of a mid-sized city. James Blake had been chief for the past twelve years. His office was located in a modern building overlooking the main body of the lake on its western side. His view was picture perfect, with sails from yacht club boats adding a swish of color to a gray lake. I explained who I was, and the nature of my interest. He warmed up and gave me several additional details.

"We assume that he was attempting to land at the Madison Airport, somehow lost control, and landed in the reservoir, about a hundred yards out from Main Harbor Marina," explained the chief. The Madison Airport is a small, one runway, suburban airfield just north of Jackson. "The plane came out of the water an hour ago. It appears from paperwork found inside the plane that the pilot was going to the Canton Flea Market next Thursday. We found a booth registration in the name of Watson Clocks. The biggest problem that we are having is locating a body."

"It wasn't strapped in the plane?" I asked.

"No sir," he replied. "We cannot find a body."

"Isn't that somewhat unusual?" I asked, knowing the answer to the question.

"Damned unusual. Those divers out there are the best," he said, pointing out his picture window. "We'll keep looking for another day or two." He leaned forward. "Confidentially, I don't think there is a body to be found."

I promised to keep in touch. Walking outside to the parking lot, I recalled having heard of the Canton Flea Market but had never been to the event. My girlfriend, on the other hand, thinks it's the greatest shopping experience that can be had. She is a high-powered lawyer who forsakes the legal world and takes vacation leave to shop in Canton on the second Thursday in May and October. I got into my 1968 Camaro and headed north up Interstate 55 toward Canton. I had the feeling that I was about to discover a lot about the Canton Flea Market.

Chapter 2

Leaving the heavy traffic and clogged shopping areas of northeast Jackson, I cruised north on Interstate 55 in my Camaro, windows down and air rushing through the interior. Just past the Natchez Trace Parkway, the posted highway speed changed to seventy miles per hour. I inched the speedometer up accordingly, and watched the gently rolling countryside slide by. It would take less than fifteen minutes to travel to Canton.

Within a few miles, I encountered a billboard advertising Canton as a good place to stop and shop. The sign also pointed out that the city was a good place if one has some "time to kill," a reference to the movie bearing the same words.

"A Time To Kill" was filmed in Canton in the fall of 1995, made its local premiere on July 13, 1996, and was released nationwide July 24. The movie, based on the novel by John Grisham, grossed over $53 million during its first four weeks of release. The gross went to over $100 million after eight weeks, and the film finished 1996 in ninth place for gross receipts. When Grisham sold the movie rights, he stipulated that he would have approval over the script and much of the cast. His presence was constant during the filming, and dozens of local citizens had bit parts in the movie. The sound stage built for the occasion is now a point of interest for tourists who visit the area.

Taking the Canton exit and driving a few more blocks, I found myself in the heart of downtown, which is to say, the Square. Someday, I imagine, a real estate developer will replicate the beauty of the Square in Canton, as the central feature in a gigantic shopping mall or some New Urbanism residential project. Such a task would be folly because it would not be real. The influences on the Square from the surrounding area would be missing. It would be like taking a mixture of sugar, salt and pepper, and removing the sugar and expecting the remaining potion to be indistinguishable from the original. It just does not work that way. To really experience the Square, one must come to the Square.

I found the organization that puts on the Flea Market in a two-story building overlooking the Square. My

purpose was to learn all I could about Watson Clocks. I went inside and was greeted by an attractive young woman who could not have been more than nineteen years old. I told her that I needed some information about one of the exhibitors. She handed me a newspaper tabloid of some twenty pages.

"The exhibitors and their booth locations are listed in here," she said with a smile. "Please feel free to keep that copy."

"What about the people who actually rent the booths? Do you have any information about them?"

She eyed me curiously and said, "You would need to talk to Ms. Devine about that. She is the event manager." She looked at her wristwatch. "She's at a meeting now. I suggest you come back in about an hour and a half. She should be back by then."

"Well, I guess that I have some 'time to kill' in Canton," I said with a grin.

She sensed my dilemma, and immediately came to the rescue by saying, "You could do some shopping on the Square, or if you like history, you could do a walking tour of historic homes in the area." She handed me a small booklet. "This is a guidebook that has a route and a description of the buildings you will see. It should take you about an hour and a half. Ms. Devine should be here when you get back. Just bring back the booklet—it's out of print."

I promised to do so, and set out on the walking tour. The booklet informed me that Canton was the county seat of Madison County, which was named for James Madison, the fourth President of the United States.

Madison County is Mississippi's twenty-third county and was created in 1828. It has often been called "The Land Between Two Rivers," because of its boundaries—the Big Black River on the northwest and the Pearl River on the southeast.

In 1836, the City of Canton was incorporated after having been determined by government-hired surveyors to be the geographical center of the county. Four hundred hearty souls who had settled in the area called it home. Any new city needs laws to govern the conduct of its citizenry and visitors. The content of such laws is usually governed by the times. In Canton's case, the first law placed on the books was an ordinance making it a misdemeanor to gallop a horse, mare or mule on any street or alley. In only two years, entrepreneurs established successful, growing businesses, including two banks, two hotels, ten dry goods stores, a drugstore, three groceries, a bakery, a tin shop, a livery stable, three tailor shops, and two watchmakers. On the public side, a courthouse, a church, and a female academy added to the collection of nonresidential buildings. Cotton was "King," and the wealth it helped to create resulted in the construction of a number of beautiful homes.

I began my tour at the intersection of Center and North Liberty Streets, heading east on Center Street. The booklet described most of the significant buildings. A few caught my eye. At 237 East Center was a classic little building with Ionic columns. Historians believe it was moved from the nearby town of Sharon just before the Civil War, to another location in Canton, and then

moved to its present site. It has been used as an office by a dentist who was killed in the Civil War, a male academy, a studio for a violin teacher, a beauty parlor, an art museum, a family residence, a bank building and a lawyer's office.

One of the most beautiful houses in Canton is located at 239 East Center Street. An imposing Italianate Renaissance structure built in 1834 around a small dog trot house, one of its outstanding features is its "Captain's Walk," and gold sphere finial. On the pillars of the garden gate are cannonballs brought from the battlefields of Vicksburg after the Civil War. There is a beautiful formal garden featuring boxwoods, camellias, and brick walkways. At one time the garden was featured on many Mississippi postcards. In the backyard are a kitchen, a carriage house, and a stone cistern house.

At 261 East Center Street is one of the glories of Canton which has been inhabited by the Mosby family since 1878. It is a Greek Revival mansion that was begun in 1852 by Colonel Wiley Lyon, who planned it to be an in-town plantation house, hence the cupola for overseeing the fields to the north. Before departing for Europe to purchase furnishings and marble mantles, Colonel Lyon gave detailed plans to the builder for a wide, walnut staircase to the second floor. He left no plans for ascension to the third floor, so the builder did not make a way to that level. He then personally supervised the installation of a spiral stairway. Work progressed slowly on the structure, with its twenty spacious rooms, mortared walls, massive Corinthian columns, forty-foot hallways, intricately carved pediment, and huge rear wings enclosing a courtyard. Mr. Mosby, a large landowner, planter and operator of Mississippi's oldest family-owned drug store, purchased the house from the first owner. Inside the home are many beautiful pieces of furniture.

Down the street at 342 East Center Street is the Howell House. According to my booklet, it is over one hundred fifty years old. It is a board and batten bungalow that was moved from Sharon before the Civil War. The cypress boards are hand sawed, and when foundation work was done on the house in the 1950s, it was discovered that the huge timbers underneath were held together with cypress pegs that are two feet long. At that time, the sixteen-foot ceilings were lowered for warmth, and one can see where the carpenter replaced the original long, narrow windows because they were too tall for the lowered ceilings. It was also at that time that the cisterns were filled in. Before the days of running water, all homes had cisterns to catch the runoff of rainwater from the gutters. It was not until 1893 that the town voted on a plant "to manufacture electricity and to distribute water."

This cottage was the turn of the century residence of Dr. John B. Howell and his widowed mother, "Miss Blanche," a beloved town character who loved to remember her aristocratic English heritage. When the concrete drive was installed, the contractors unearthed a silver teapot that Miss Blanche used to water her ferns. Widowed just before the death of her only child, Miss Blanche was very close to her son, and followed him to Jackson when he went to Millsaps College. A lover of books, she helped organize the Millsaps Library and became the first full-time college librarian.

The opposite vacant lot was once the site of the Harvey House, an imposing two-story frame house. George Harvey was once mayor of Canton, and Captain Addison Harvey organized and led the intrepid Harvey Scouts, a famous Madison County unit during the Civil War. They scouted the Mississippi River, and also followed Sherman with guerrilla skirmishes. There is a unique monument on the south side of East Academy Street erected in honor of the brave slaves who served with the Harvey Scouts. It was erected in the 1890s by

19

William Howcutt, who later moved to New Orleans. Howcutt also made a contribution to a church in Canton on behalf of the freed slaves.

The booklet instructed me to turn south onto Madison Street, then to stop at Peace Street and consider two more houses. One of them was 504 East Peace Street. The house was begun in 1847, but of more interest was the story behind the namesake of the house. The name Smith-Vaniz is well-known in central Mississippi, but what is not so well-known is how the name originated. Dr. George Washington Smith was constantly having his mail mixed up with another Cantonian named George Washington Smith. It was irritating for both men, so Dr. Smith decided to do something about it. He placed all the letters of the alphabet in a hat and had each of his five children draw one letter. The word VANIZ was made from the letters, and legally added to the family name.

I turned west on East Peace Street and walked upon a familiar-looking house. After consulting my guide, I realized that I had seen this house on television before. Because of its picturesque beauty and its carvings and spindles, it has been the backdrop for several television commercials. Known as the Vanity Castle, it is located at 440 East Peace Street. It was built by Judge Will Powell for his beautiful wife, Amanda, and among other things, was known for its intercom system, which was a first in the state.

The handsome Neo-classical residence at 379 East Peace Street was built in 1906. It contains thirteen fireplaces, each with a mantle of different design.

The Shackleford House at 326 East Peace Street also caught my attention. I paused and read its story in the guidebook.

This beautiful Georgian gem was begun in 1849 and finished in 1852 for Col. Charles Clark Shackleford, one of the county's most outstanding men. He was judge of a ten-county district and President of the Mississippi Central Railroad. To celebrate the completion of their home, the Shacklefords gave a huge housewarming party and served venison, barbecued sheep and steers stuffed with quail.

The mellowed brick walls are over a foot thick—mortared on each side. Each of the ten original rooms is 20 x 20 with 16 foot ceilings downstairs. Originally, the front rooms were twin parlors and the original furniture and draperies are still in the west room. Also, Judge Shackleford's personal law library has been kept intact.

During his invasion of Canton, Sherman set up his headquarters across the street under the big oak tree in the front yard. Throughout the South, Sherman stayed in a tent that was patrolled all night long by two Union soldiers, because he didn't trust those Rebels enough to stay in one of their houses. (For years afterward, the landmark tree was known as the Sherman Oak.) The Shackleford mansion was commandeered for a hospital for wounded soldiers.

Family members repeat this story: When one of the Southern women who was acting as a nurse for the wounded Yankees was molested by a soldier, Dr. Booth, an attending Southern physician, moved to stop him and was shot and killed on the back porch by another soldier.

Judge Shackleford's historical prominence in developing a railroad system to move the state's cotton was remembered when the Illinois Central celebrated its Hundredth Anniversary, and his grandsons were invited to represent him as dignitaries.

Through the years, young family members and their friends have enjoyed prowling the attic for all the Confederate uniforms and other war treasures stored there, as well as taking the risk of confronting the attic ghost. Only a few years ago, a great grandson retrieved from under the eaves, a Yankee sword still wrapped in the cloth in which it had been hidden.

The house at 313 East Peace is over one hundred years old, and is the subject of another Civil War tale. It seems that during the occupation of Canton during the Civil War, Dr. and Mrs. A. H. Cage lived in this house and had a small baby. When Sherman's troops took Canton, they also took all of the livestock in sight, including the cow from this residence. Mrs. Cage bravely visited Union headquarters and demanded return of the cow for her child. The commanding officer apparently was moved to grant her request, but told her to keep the cow "close." The protective mother kept the cow in her bedroom on the east side of her house for five whole days and nights—until the Yankees left.

The guidebook took me on a weave through even more streets of historic houses and places. I never realized Canton had so much history, especially when compared to Jackson. Of course, Jackson was burned more than once during the Civil War, and was even known as Chimneyville. Back at the Square, I surveyed the scene before me—a beautiful courthouse surrounded by buildings over a hundred years old, most of which had been restored, in use by thriving businesses. As I gazed at the buildings on the east side of the Square, I did a double-take when I discovered a coffin on the upper facade of one of the buildings. I made a mental note to tell my girlfriend, Laura, to look for the coffin on the Square when she came to the Flea Market.

I went back to my point of origin, and found that Ms. Devine had also returned, and had been told of my inquiry. She was a young sixty-year old, with a crown of thick, silver hair. I explained to her that I was attempting to locate the Watson Clock owners in reference to the plane crash. She acted as if she understood my situation.

"Let me just check my registrations here," she said as she rifled through a full file jacket. "Watson Clocks is one of our more popular exhibitors. Larry and Wanda Watson are the operators. They are from Florida. They will be in a booth on East Fulton Street this year, right across from the Old Jail. I suppose I should say that she will be in the booth. What a strong woman."

Chapter 3

When I travel out of town for any significant distance, I always rent a car from an agency instead of driving my Camaro. The 1968 gem of an automobile is fully restored and is as reliable as a car that age can be. Nevertheless, it would be very inconvenient to break down in rural Mississippi and not have readily available parts. So Saturday morning found me at a local rental car company's front door when it opened for business. I wanted something small and sporty. The best they could do was a new Buick Riviera. It wasn't small, but it was sporty enough. The luxury didn't hurt, either.

Destin, Florida, is a fairly easy five-hour drive from Jackson. One takes Highway 49 to Hattiesburg, then US 98 over to Mobile, where a connection is made with Interstate 10. My favorite route is to continue on I-10 and bypass the Pensacola area. With the construction of the Mid-Bay Bridge several years ago, it is a more convenient route. The road becomes a causeway, twenty feet above the water on concrete pilings. Halfway across the bay the roadway rises some forty or fifty feet to allow tall-masted boats to pass beneath.

I paid the toll at the Mid-Bay Bridge tollbooth and started across the bridge, eyeing a developing thunderstorm dead ahead. Had I been in a boat, I would have stayed in dock until the storm passed. But in a car, I figured I would be across the bay before it grew and did any damage. I was wrong.

About a third of the way across the concrete span, it was obvious that I would not get across the bay before the storm was on top of the bridge. That was not of great concern. People drive into thunderstorms everyday. It just so happened that I was on a highway over water, instead of a highway over land. I noticed that there were no cars in my lane heading south. There were three heading north in the opposite lane. At the highest point on the bridge ahead, I could distinguish the blackening sky. Just as I was about to reach the rising part of the bridge, the gusts of wind grew to angry speeds. The Riviera swayed side to side and felt like it was being slowed as if caught in a giant spider web. I was faced with the choice of reducing my speed and being at the top of the bridge when the worst of it hit, or increasing my speed and running the risk of being blown into the concrete guard rail. I chose the middle ground and reduced speed sparingly. The car was almost bucking as I reached the top of the bridge. As I started down the opposite side, the sky turned from dark gray to pitch black, and lightning streaked out to the sides. The thunder came less than a second later, and boomed in my ears. Suddenly, hailstones the size of peas rained down on the car, and for the first time I felt that I was in imminent danger. Stopping on the bridge did not seem like a good idea, so I crawled ahead at twenty-five miles per hour. The hail stopped suddenly, and then raindrops the size of marbles lashed at the car. It was as if a wall of water was cascading down on the car. All I was doing was holding on. I turned on the windshield wipers as fast as they would go, yet still could barely see the road ahead. This lasted for only three or four minutes, then ended as quickly as it had begun. I looked ahead and saw palm trees and bushes. In my rearview mirror the torrent was still raging. I said a silent prayer for any other cars that might be on the bridge. My heart was pounding as I took a deep breath and kept going.

I drove to the Destin Airport and spotted the Avion Flying Service immediately, thanks to a large sign on the side of its hangar. The airfield ramp was one-quarter filled with small planes of vacationers down for the weekend. During the summer season, the place would be packed with planes. I parked in the visitors' lot and went inside the hangar to a small office area. A middle-aged man was sitting behind a gray metal desk, wearing a tee shirt that proclaimed "Learn To Fly." He greeted me, and I explained who I was, and handed him a copy of the morning's Jackson newspaper. He looked at the color photo on the front page. It depicted his plane being pulled out of the muddy water of a lake he did not know existed. He stared at it momentarily, then slammed it down on his desk.

"Damn him!" He looked up at the ceiling, calming himself. "I'm sorry. That was uncalled for. How can I help you?"

"Tell me about Larry Watson," I said.

"Larry Watson," he said slowly, considering his words before he spoke. "A creep, a huckster, and a damn good pilot."

"Is that your plane?" I asked.

"Yep. Larry came in and rented it Tuesday. Said he would pay me when he returned. He was going up to the big flea market in Canton, Mississippi. I think he made his year at that deal. Said it was the best flea market and arts and craft show in the Southeast."

"Did he rent from you often?"

"He would rent that plane about once every two months to go cross-country somewhere. Always paid late, but always paid."

"What time of day did he rent the plane?" I asked.

"Early," he said, referring to a journal on the desk. "Let's see. He rented it at seven-forty a.m., and took off immediately thereafter for Jackson, Mississippi."

"How long does it take to fly to Jackson?"

"In that plane, about two hours or so," he said.

"Any idea why he would not arrive until after ten o'clock that night?" I asked.

"Now that is a good question."

We conversed a while longer, and I left the airport with the feeling that something more was involved than just an accident. My next stop was the home of Larry Watson. I went to the local Visitors' Center and picked up a city map of Destin. Watson and his wife lived on a curbless street in the middle of town, with no water view at all. It was strictly middle-income, cookie-cutter houses. Most of them had Florida rooms, those screened-in rooms that serve as patio and porch rolled into one.

The Watson house was painted a color that was somewhere between teal and turquoise. At the edge of the backyard was an outbuilding that was almost as big as the house. I presumed it was the cuckoo clock manufacturing center. There was a red Toyota parked in the carport. I rang the doorbell and waited an appropriate length of time, then rang it again. I did this two more times. Finally, I knocked loudly on the door.

"Nobody's home, mister," said an elderly voice from next door. "They're gone to a show until next week. She left this afternoon; he left a few days ago." It was a lady in her late sixties who was sweeping her driveway. I thanked her and drove off. I would have to catch up with Mrs. Watson in Canton.

I checked into a beachside motel, where rates were down forty percent from a month ago. I was just in time to spend twenty minutes with a Gulf of Mexico sunset that painted the sky a dozen shades of blue, red and orange. When the sun kissed the water, I could almost hear it.

Whether it was because of the sunset, or a flyer in the motel lobby announcing the grand opening of a new art shop at the local outlet center, I do not really know. Perhaps it was a combination of both that put me in a mood for art appreciation. This was a new experience for me. As a cop for twenty years, I had not given much thought to the art world. Whatever the reason, I headed over to the new shop. It was named Vibrant Colors and was at the end of the newest strip of buildings in the ever-expanding shopping center of upscale manufacturers' outlets, which sold at deeply-discounted prices. Upon entering the gallery-store I was handed a glass of white wine in a two-piece, put-together, plastic wine glass and, in a gravelly voice, invited by a suntanned middle-aged woman with orange lipstick and platinum hair to ". . . enjoy browsing around tonight. We are featuring artists from Mississippi, Alabama and the

Florida Panhandle this month, and everything is on sale, honey."

The first thing I noticed about the artwork was that the prices seemed outrageously high. But then again, I didn't know anything about art. The second thing I noticed was a pattern. The Florida artists painted sea oats and sand dunes, the Alabama artists favored big oak trees and hanging moss, and the Mississippi artists preferred country roads. There was one notable exception to the Mississippi artists. Emerald Greene's paintings were of flowers and flower gardens. As I admired one of her six displayed paintings, I was approached by an attractive woman about my age. She wore a long dress.

"She does excellent work, doesn't she?"

"Yes," was all I could say. I did not want to add some additional comment that might show my ignorance.

"Emerald lives and works in Canton, Mississippi. We are honored to be representing her in Florida," she gushed. "Please let me know if you have any further interest."

I assured her that I would, then drifted from one painting to the next with the crowd, which was two-thirds tourists and one-third local folks. Besides the art on display, it seemed that the main topic of conversation was a major jewel heist earlier in the week from the Sandhorn Center, a local, privately-owned museum.

The next morning I got up at eight o'clock, jogged five miles along the beach to keep my one-hundred eighty-eight-pound body in shape and then drove back to Jackson. There was only one message on my answering machine.

"I am a friend. You will find the answers that you need in one of the houses in Canton known to have a ghost."

The voice was that of a white female in her mid- to late twenties. I played the message over several times trying to pick up a clue about the background noise, but there was nothing that helped identify where she was calling from. With all of my high-tech computer and electronic equipment, I have yet to install a simple caller I.D. device that would allow me to discover who called, and from what number. I pulled out a little pad and made a note to have it installed.

So, who would know which houses in Canton have ghosts? I suppose Ms. Devine would be a good place to start. I would call her first thing in the morning.

Chapter 4

A ghost is, first and foremost, the spirit of a dead person. There are supposedly good ghosts and bad ghosts. The bad ghosts are usually from a person who died before his or her time, often as the victim of some crime. Such a ghost is bent on revenge, or making someone else's life miserable.

When I was a young boy, my friends and I would go to an old, abandoned house in a rural area not far from a river. The house had no windows or doors, just floors, walls and a roof. It was an old house; the interior walls were unfinished boards. There was only one room on the second floor, and it had a dormer. It was in the dormer that the ghost would appear. Legend had it that the owner of the property was hung one night by a group of outlaws who heard that the man had comforted an outcast family in a nearby town. His spirit would appear in the dormer whenever a rope was thrown over a large, low-hanging branch of the massive oak tree in the front yard.

One night, when I was a sophomore in high school, two of my buddies and I went to that house and threw a rope over that branch. What happened next is hard to describe. All I can say is that we heard a noise in the house. One friend would later describe it as an agonizing scream. The other friend said it was the scream of a young child. I prayed it was a cat. Anyway, at the time of the scream, one of my friends shined his flashlight up in the oak tree, and a shadow appeared in the window. It was not a shadow on a wall, but a shadow of a man "in" the window—a three-dimensional shadow, if you will. I don't know what it was, but it scared me like I have never been scared before—or since. I was so scared that my hair hurt.

Today, Ms. Devine of the Canton Flea Market would be my source on ghosts. She answered on the first ring, and I explained to her that I was also interested in some of the ghosts of Canton.

"I hope you have a lot of time," she grinned over the telephone. "We have plenty of ghosts in Canton."

"Yes. I got that impression from my walking tour the other day. Would you care to name the three most prominent ghosts?"

"That's easy. The most well-known are in the Mosby House, the Priestly House, and the Greene Mansion."

"I have an unusual favor to ask of you, Ms. Devine," I said seriously. "I collect ghost stories. I would like to visit those houses. May I say that you referred me?"

"I'll do better than that," she replied. "I'll inform the owners that you will be calling on them."

I thanked her, and noted those three places on a pad. An hour later, I was cruising up East Center Street, attempting to recall the Mosby House from my walking tour earlier. I found the house and walked up the sidewalk to the porch with its four massive columns. I rang the doorbell and waited. After several attempts, it was obvious that no one was home. I walked back to my car, and was greeted by a grandmother-type as I opened the car door.

"They are out of town today," she said with authority. "Can I help you?"

"No. I don't think so. I was just searching for some information about the house."

"I can tell you anything you want to know," she said. "Everybody knows about everybody else's house. This is Canton."

"I see," I said. "What I'm interested in are ghosts."

I waited for her cynical laugh, but instead she said seriously, "Well, you have come to the right place. There is at least one in that house. Maybe more."

"Do tell."

"Both ghosts—if indeed there are two ghosts—are good ghosts. Personally, I think there is only one ghost. He just is different from time to time. He started making appearances over a hundred years ago. He's what one might call a cute, twinkly little fellow. He wears gray, and is supposed to appear to people who are in danger of dying. Fortunately, nobody has seen him lately, and nobody has died, either."

"And what about the other one?"

"It's probably the same one," she said with a grin and a nod of her head. "They don't see that one. They just see evidence of where he has been. You know, like you walk into a room and a chair will be rocking, as if someone has just gotten up from it."

"When will the Mosbys be home?"

"Oh, it will be two or three more days," she said. "They are off on vacation."

"Where did they go?"

"Destin," she said.

Chapter 5

If I were a ghost, I would be a friendly ghost. Friendly ghosts are helpful, and, more often, died a natural death. Marley, the ghost in *A Christmas Carol* by Charles Dickens, was a helpful ghost. He helped Scrooge become a better man. I would also choose to live in the Priestly House. But it's unlikely that I could reside there, because it is already the home of a friendly ghost. I drove a few blocks to that location, and parked on the side of the street.

The Priestly House is located at 138 East Fulton Street. It is owned by a woman who purchased it at an auction and restored it to showcase condition. She was sitting on the front porch in a white wicker rocking chair as I walked through the waist-high, wrought iron gate. I explained to her that I had been referred by Ms. Devine, and that I was collecting ghost stories. She was only too happy to show me around and show off her new home. She introduced herself as Nora Panella. She was an enchanting woman in her early forties, with shoulder-length golden hair and long manicured fingernails. She wore a fashionable pants suit and a gold chain necklace.

We went inside the massive front door to a foyer with a staircase and large rooms on both sides. We walked into the high-ceilinged chamber on the left, and she began telling me about the history of the home. Her soft voice had the flavor of a knowledgeable museum tour guide who was devoted to her work.

"It was built in 1852 by Dr. James Priestly. Legend claims he rode into Canton on horseback and became the town doctor and postmaster. The house was built with hand-hewn cypress and heart pine. Originally, it was only one room deep and two stories tall, with a large center hallway. The staircase we passed is hand-turned walnut, and leads to the two second-story bedrooms and portico. I'll tell you more about that staircase in a minute. This was their living room. I'm told that there was a cellar under this floor, and that on bitter cold winter days, the servants would go there to catch the warmth from the fireplace. The fireplace serves not only this room, but the bedroom directly above this one. During the Civil War, Dr. Priestly's youngest son, Charles, was too young to join the Confederate Army, so he stayed here and ran the place. Can you just see a fourteen-year-old boy as the man of this house? His name was Charles, and at fifteen he went to work as flagman and freight conductor on the railroad because of the manpower shortage. He went on to become a doctor, and was later the town hero during a yellow fever epidemic, when all the other doctors were either gone or victims themselves of the terrible fever."

"Is he the ghost?" I asked.

"Oh no," she replied. "Topsy is the ghost."

"Topsy?"

"Yes. She was one of the descendants who lived here during the Depression. The house had many additions, as you will see," she said as we walked into a formal dining room. "In 1912 they added this formal dining hall and double parlor, then a latticed hall that led to the outside kitchen." We walked through a hallway to the back of the house. "Later, they added three more bedrooms and enclosed the two-story back porch. Topsy converted this big old house into a rooming house and took in boarders. Naturally, times were tough and everybody did what they had to do. But Topsy kept her sense of style. It is said that she served those boarders as if they were her best friends. She even used the elegant china and embroidered napkins."

"And how does she appear these days?" I asked.

"Let's go upstairs," she said.

We made our way to the second floor, up a back stairway and finally into her bedroom, which had a large master bathroom suite off to the rear. This room was directly above the living room where we had started the tour. The fireplace was against the outside wall of the room. Her room was as fine as any interior designer could create, and the room alone, much less the house, would make an excellent feature story in a fine homes magazine.

"This is where I live," she said.

"It's beautiful."

"Thank you," she responded. "I almost moved out the first week I was here. I had just gotten to bed after setting the security system and was just about asleep when I heard three knocks on my door. Not my outside door, but the door to my bedroom. Someone was at the top of the stairs. I grabbed my bedside telephone and called the police. I told the officer what was happening, and he asked where I was calling from. When I told him the Priestly House, he told me that it was just Topsy and to go back to sleep."

"What did you do?"

"I pulled the covers over my head and went to sleep. Somehow, I just felt this comforting presence."

"I don't know if I could have done that," I said.

"Come on. Let me show you one more room." We walked out her bedroom door and across the top of the stairway to another bedroom. I should say bedroom suite. It too looked like it came out a magazine advertisement. I noticed two unusual washtubs displayed against the wall beside the fireplace.

"What are these?" I asked.

"We found those out back in one of the smaller houses," she said with a smile. "Those are bathtubs." She went over and bent down beside one of them. "Notice how much larger this one is. It's an adult tub and the other is a child's tub. See how this side comes up higher? It's for the back."

She continued pointing out the features of the room, and mentioned that her bed and breakfast guests stayed in this room. Breakfast was served downstairs. We walked back to the top of the stairs.

"You asked about ghosts," she said. "Shortly after I bought this house, I was removing some of the paint from the stair rail here at the top of the stairs. You will notice that the stair rail is walnut here and that it is a lighter color here."

I looked closely and saw what she was referring to. The rails at the top of the stairs had obviously been replaced.

"My guess is that this rail was broken," she said. "Perhaps someone even fell down to the first floor. Anyway, while I was applying the remover, a strange thing happened. When I got to the light colored railing I reached beside me to put the brush in the can of paint remover, but it had been moved to a position on the floor about six feet behind me."

"Were you the only one in the house?"

"I was," she said.

As we walked back down the stairs to the first floor, I told her that I had just one more question. "Do you know of any connection that this house or Topsy would have with the Flea Market or with Destin, Florida?"

"None that I can think of," she replied.

I shrugged and said goodbye. As I was walking across the threshold of the front door I heard a cuckoo clock make its regular sound.

"What's that?" I asked.

"Oh, that's just a cuckoo clock."

"Is it an antique?"

"No. I purchased it this spring at the Flea Market. There is a booth that sells nothing but cuckoo clocks."

Chapter 6

The next house on my list was the Greene Mansion, which was located on a large, tree-shaded lot two blocks east of the Square. Set on a small hill above street level, it would best be described as a traditional southern mansion, except that it was painted a mint green instead of white. There were four large, two-story columns on the front, a wraparound porch and balcony, and tall, dominant dark green shuttered windows. The front and side yards were lush with azalea bushes, which must surely be a sea of color in the springtime. A black wrought-iron fence encircled the property. As I walked up to the massive front door, it swung open before I could ring the bell.

"Come in. Come in," said a distinguished, silver-haired man. "We have been expecting you since that lady from the Chamber of Commerce called us this morning."

He was in his seventies, only slightly stooped in the back. He stuck out an age-spotted right hand that showed a trace of arthritis and welcomed me with a firm handshake. There was a smile on his face and the twinkle of a practical joker in his eye. He wore a striped blue and white dress shirt covered by a lightweight, dark blue cardigan sweater, gray slacks and wing-tip shoes.

"I'm George Greene," he said. "Do come in."

"Jack Boulder," I said. "Did Ms. Devine explain what I was doing?"

"Said you had a hobby of collecting ghost stories."

"That's right," I confirmed. "One of these days I am

going to write a book. But you know how that goes."

He said that he did. People are always meaning to do things. "The bank president used to give away little round pieces of wood about the size and shape of a silver dollar. Had the word 'TUIT' printed on them. When people told him they were going to do something when they got around to it, he would give them one of those wooden pieces and tell them that they now had gotten a round tuit."

We both laughed at the story, which I suspect he had told often.

I surveyed the huge living room. The ceiling was at least fifteen feet high. The room was furnished with four velvet-covered sofas, two coffee tables, several end tables, period accessories, and a twenty-four light chandelier. Paintings on the wall included a landscape scene, a man on a horse, and a large matriarchal portrait over the fireplace mantle. The room appeared to be about sixteen by twenty feet.

"You have a beautiful house," I said as I craned my neck looking around.

"Thank you. It's a tough job to keep up, though. It was built in 1850. Believe it or not, it only has six rooms. Bathrooms excepted, of course."

"Really?"

"Downstairs, there are only four rooms: This living room, a formal dining room on the front side and a kitchen and art studio, which run across the full width of the house on the back side."

We walked through a door to the rear, and took one step down into the art studio, a wide room with tall ceiling and windows on two sides. On the other end was the kitchen. It was huge, and had been updated. There was the usual kitchen area at one end, a large island counter in the middle, and an informal dining area at the opposite end.

"Come on upstairs, and I'll show you the bedrooms."

It was back through the living room, then up the six-foot wide stairs to the second floor. Sure enough, there were only two bedrooms, each gargantuan in size and identical, with bathroom suites. From the clothes and furnishings, clearly a man lived in one bedroom and a woman in the other. Both rooms had fifteen-foot ceilings and were full of light from large windows. I could not help telling the gentleman how impressed I was with the beauty and simplicity of his home.

"Thank you for the compliment, indeed," he said. "My great-grandfather built this house, and he would be pleased to hear your words." He paused a second or two before saying, "But that is not why you came today. Let's go outside to the backyard."

As we ambled back down the stairs, I noticed that the first floor bathroom was located under the stairwell. We walked across the kitchen to a back door, which the old man opened with great flair. He took one step out onto the back porch and made a presentation gesture with his right hand. "Mr. Boulder, I introduce you to the back garden and the ghost of my great-grandmother, wherever she may be."

I stood there with a chill at the base of my neck as I looked at the garden. The feeling of déjà vu was overwhelming. I had been here before. Was it in this lifetime, or another? I searched my mind for a clue, but was unable to find one. At that moment, I thought I felt the wisp of someone passing beside me. Whether I believe in ghosts or not is immaterial, but something was going on.

"Are you all right, Mr. Boulder?"

"I . . . I'm fine," I said, shaking off the uncomfortable feeling. "It's such a beautiful garden."

"Oh, but you should see it in the springtime. It takes your breath away. The whole yard is awash with color. People ride by when the azaleas are in bloom, just to look. We are pleased to do this for the community," he said with pride.

As I sought to understand what was happening to me, I asked about the ghost. Maybe there was more to this than I had originally believed.

"My great-grandmother adored flowers," he said. "She planted this garden and chose the flowers so that something would be in bloom nearly every day of the year. One of the things that she loved to do each day was to cut a few flowers and put them in a vase on the mantle in the living room. Let's go back inside," he said turning toward the house. We walked back to the living room. He now stood in front of the fireplace mantle. He pointed to a dark green, cut glass vase about twelve inches high centered on the mantle. "There, as you see, is the vase. It is empty now, as it is most of the time. But about once every two months, the vase will be full full of fresh flowers from the garden when we come downstairs for breakfast in the morning."

"How long has this been happening?" I asked.

"It began about six months after she died, which was

in 1895. According to family legend, there were fresh flowers in the vase every morning. It fell off to once a week after the turn of the century, and then only sporadically after 1950, which I think is significant, because the house was one hundred years old that year."

"Pardon me for asking this question, but I feel that I must," I said apologetically.

"Do I believe in ghosts?"

"Well . . .," I stammered.

"It's a logical question, and one that I have spent a great deal of time contemplating," he said. "It is difficult to say with absolute certainty that ghosts exist. On the other hand, it is impossible to be intellectually honest and say that ghosts do not exist. Don't you agree?"

"Yes. That's very logical," I said.

"It therefore becomes strictly a matter of belief. When we talk about beliefs, we tread on very dangerous ground. For example, many people who believe in heaven and hell think it is absolutely foolish for people to believe in ghosts. Yet, they believe that the devil is real, and at work in the world today. So let me put it this way—there is evidence of a so-called ghost in this house. The evidence is rather compelling."

"Have there been any efforts made to document her presence? You know—hidden cameras, et cetera?"

"Through the years there have been many attempts to physically verify her existence. Cameras, trip wires and such have all been tried. Great-grandmother just goes right through them. I don't know about believing in ghosts in general, but I know that my great-grandmother is still here. And we appreciate the flowers."

There was little more left to say. I thanked Mr. Greene, and left the Greene Mansion with a mixture of emotions. He had gotten rather dramatic toward the end. Maybe the years were catching up to him. In any case, I still could not get over the strange feeling I had when I first saw that garden. Had I seen a ghost without knowing it?

Chapter 7

I motored back to Jackson on Interstate 55 and arrived at my condo in time for the five-thirty national news. It was the same old stuff—political corruption, a third-world country in distress, and a wrap-up with news that Americans could use to improve their lives. Whatever happened to Walter Cronkite?

The six o'clock local news was somewhat better. Crime was going down, and a large corporation announced it would move its new headquarters to an industrial park in Madison County. There was a feature story on the preparations for the Canton Flea Market. In sports news, all eight Mississippi universities were undefeated after three weeks into the current football season. No one was celebrating, however, since they all had played the worst teams on their schedules.

As the television meteorologist was giving tomorrow's forecast, the telephone beside me rang. I immediately thought about that caller identification system and realized I needed to do that tomorrow. I answered with a simple hello. It was the young woman again. The friend.

"Did you connect anything in Destin with your visit to Canton today?" she said.

"What do you mean?" I answered, as I turned on a device that would record the conversation without her knowledge. In Mississippi, recording a telephone conversation is not illegal if one person is aware of the recording device.

"What big event happened in Destin this past week?"

"How should I know?" I said. "I was only there for one night."

"Look, stupid," she intoned. "Connect the big story in Destin with the haunted house in Canton, and you can solve your case. Now get to it, big boy."

She hung up and left me sitting there feeling like the odd man out. What did the rest of the world know that I did not know? Wait—there was a Destin newspaper in my overnight bag. I had stashed it there intending to read it upon my return, but had gotten involved with my haunted house hunting in Canton. And who was this woman telling me what to look for in my investigation? She obviously had some self-interest. I went to the closet and found the travel bag. Sure enough, tucked in the side pocket was last Thursday's edition of the town's weekly newspaper. I devoured the article on the front page.

On Monday evening, the Sandhorn Museum was burglarized and one of its most valuable pieces, a sixty carat emerald, was stolen. The theft occurred sometime between 11:30 p.m. and 7:00 a.m., according to Captain James Grimes of Nightwatch Patrol Services, the company that provides security to the museum.

The theft was discovered at 7:00 a.m. when a Nightwatch security guard made a routine check and found the emerald and its display case missing. Grimes said that the electric power to the building had been shut off at the breaker box, and he was at a loss as to why the security alarm did not sound. He declined to discuss further details, citing security reasons; however, it had been learned that the building has no on-site security personnel after 11:00 p.m.

The Sandhorn Museum is a two thousand square foot concrete block structure built in 1995 by wealthy real estate investor and art collector John Sandhorn of New York City. He owns a summer home in Destin. The emerald was a gift to his wife in 1990. Other exhibits in the museum include sculptures, paintings and jewelry collected by Sandhorn over his career.

The museum has faced two other major controversies in its brief existence. It met stiff opposition from local residents when it was built without a permit, and then later granted a variance. Opponents charged that it was a commercial structure that was too close to a residential neighborhood. It was also the subject of an Internal Revenue Service review after Sandhorn claimed it as a business expense. The IRS alleged that it was a private collection and not a business venture, since it was not promoted to the public. The case was settled after Sandhorn agreed to pay back taxes plus penalties and change the museum's method of operation.

Police say that their investigation is continuing.

I read the article one more time. Okay, there was a jewel heist in Destin on Monday night. Larry Watson took off in a plane for Jackson Tuesday morning, headed for the Canton Flea Market. Was that unusual? Did he usually drive with his wife? Where was Larry Watson during the several hours between the time he left Tuesday morning, and the time of the plane crash Tuesday night? I agreed that it was worth checking out.

What was the connection to a house with a ghost in Canton? Who was my mystery caller, anyway? I mentally retraced my drive to Destin, my visit to the airport, the motel, and the art dealer.

Wait a minute! I snapped my finger. One of the artists featured at Vibrant Colors was from Canton. I remember her name because it was so unusual. Emerald Greene. The Greene Mansion in Canton. A house in Canton with a ghost. Of course. It also explained why I felt so weird when I first saw the flower garden in the back yard of the Greene Mansion! It was the same flower garden I had seen in the painting by Emerald Greene at the gallery in Destin.

Even though it was now six-forty p.m., I departed my condo immediately, and drove back to the Greene Mansion in Canton.

Chapter 8

It was dark when I arrived, and I discovered a beautiful side of Canton that is not visible in the daylight. The buildings in the downtown area were outlined by rows of lights. Hundreds of lights. For some reason, I felt like I was in a Christmas card. It is practically a scene out of a Victorian village. It reminded me of Walt Disney World when the sun goes down. Centered in this scene was the lighted courthouse. The drivers who are passing through on Interstate 55 are unaware that such a gem is only two miles off their concrete ribbon of travel.

I pulled up in front of the Greene Mansion, parked the Camaro, and studied the house. There was one light on in the upstairs woman's bedroom and light coming from the studio in back. I walked up the front steps and rang the doorbell. From inside I could hear a four-note chime.

A woman in her mid-forties answered the door, opening it just wide enough for me to see her, blocking the entrance. She was attractive in an intellectual sort of way, and had the look of a teacher about her. Perhaps it was because of her wire-rimmed glasses. Her straight hair was shoulder-length, and she wore a man's green-plaid flannel shirt, blue jeans, and a pair of brown penny loafers.

"I'm sorry to disturb you," I said. She did not respond. "Is Mr. Greene in?"

"Who are you?"

"Jack Boulder," I replied. "I met Mr. Greene this afternoon and I . . ."

"Wait here," she said, cutting me off and closing the door. A bright porch light came on over my head. A long minute later, the door reopened. This time both the woman and Mr. Greene were there. He was in front and she was standing behind him, looking over his shoulder.

"I'm Jack Boulder, Mr. Greene. I was here earlier. I'm the guy who collects ghost stories. Could I ask you just a couple more questions?"

"Come in," he said.

The three of us walked into the living room. The chandelier was now turned on, changing the character of the room. I looked up at the mantle. The green vase was still resting in wait of fresh flowers. I took more notice now of the large painting over the mantle. It was a life-sized portrait of a woman dressed in a formal summer dress, sitting primly on a wrought-iron yard chair in front of a flower garden. A gold-leaf frame wrapped around the painting's rectangular edges. No doubt the flower garden in the painting was the same as the one in the back yard. Then I noticed it—a gold necklace, perhaps three-quarters of an inch wide, lay around her neck. Set in the necklace was a large emerald.

"Is that your great-grandmother in the painting?" I asked as they joined me in gazing up at the matriarch.

"Yes. That's her," replied Mr. Greene. "She was quite a lady. She is the one who started the flower garden. As you can see from the empty vase, she did not bring us any flowers tonight." He took a step closer to the mantle. "Of course, that is not unusual. She usually gathers the flowers early in the morning."

The old man seemed to be drifting, perhaps reflecting. It was not senility or old age. This gentleman still had all of his faculties. Emerald Greene took a step forward and said, "What is it that you want, Mr. . . ., what was it? Boulder?"

What I really wanted was to take off this pretense of being a collector of ghost stories, and put on my investigator hat. I wanted to tell them that a large, valuable emerald had been stolen a few days ago from a private museum in Destin, Florida. I wanted to tell them that I was conducting an investigation into a mysterious plane crash. I wanted to ask this artist about her connection with

Destin. What I wanted was to stop pretending. Unfortunately, I knew what would happen if I revealed my true identity and mission at this point. They would invite me to get back in my cute little car and drive back to wherever I came from. So I continued the charade. Maybe I could work in the questions that I wanted answered.

"I'm sorry," I said. "Ms. Greene, is it?"

She just stared at me. A cold stare. The kind in which the muscles around the eyes are tightened. It was the kind of stare that sent a message. It told me that she was skeptical of my visit and my inquiries.

"I'm just trying to find out as much as I can about this lady," I said, opening my palm in gesture to the painting.

I detected a change in her demeanor all of a sudden. It was slight, but evident. It had gone from skepticism to annoyance. As she turned to walk away, she said to her father, "I'll be in the studio."

After she left the room the old man said, "You will have to excuse Emerald. She is rather high-strung. You know how artists can be sometimes."

"Is your daughter Emerald Greene, the famous artist?"

He smiled and said, "Well, she is beginning to get a little fame. But she has a ways to go." He looked up at the painting again. "In case you haven't guessed, she was named after that," he said, pointing to the painting.

"Your great-grandmother?"

"No. The necklace. The emerald."

Of course. Emerald Greene. The question was begging to be asked so I obliged.

"What is so special about that necklace?"

"Let's go sit down, and I will tell you," he said, and then led me to a plush sofa which I immediately sunk into. He pulled a chair closer. "That necklace is very special. My great-grandfather bought it in Colombia, South America in 1858. He was what you might call a broker, someone who puts buyers and sellers together. If a farmer in Mississippi wanted the best price for his cotton, Thomas Madison Greene was the best man to find a buyer. If a steamboat company in Vicksburg needed a loan, he could find a bank that would lend the money. He was well-connected. He was also a wheeler, a dealer, and a traveler. He made things happen. Lots of people in Canton wondered where he got his money, because he did not make it around here. All that most of them knew was that he would get on a train at the railroad station, and not come back for a month or two."

"He must have accumulated quite a fortune," I observed.

"That he did. But he wound up losing most of it." He paused. "Would you care for a cup of tea? The water was just reaching a boil when you arrived."

I accepted his offer without hesitation, and he got up slowly and went toward the kitchen. He made a gesture that indicated he had more to say. The worst thing I could do now would be to interrupt. I learned a long time ago, during questioning of suspects, that it was best to let a talker talk. Mr. Greene returned with a silver serving tray containing two china cups, a small silver pitcher of steaming hot water, and small containers of cream and sugar. Several tea bags of undetermined origin rested on the tray. We took the cups and tea bags and continued the conversation.

"This probably seems unusual to you, Mr. Boulder," he said, dipping a tea bag in a steaming cup of hot water. "We southerners usually drink iced tea instead of hot tea." I mumbled a polite response and he continued with the story of his great-grandfather.

"As I was saying, he bought that emerald for his wife, Eliza, and it became not only her most prized possession, but the talk of Canton. They say it changed her life because she began attending more social events, and eventually began hosting parties. She wanted to show that necklace off."

"Where is the emerald now?" I asked, as I took my first sip of hot tea. It was bitter, but I kept sipping anyway.

"It's a sad story. During the Civil War, the Union soldiers came to Canton. There was a military hospital here. Canton did not exactly put up a lot of resistance because of the overwhelming forces against it. One of the Yankee sympathizers was none other than Thomas Madison Greene. He even let the Union soldiers use this house. But, he turned into a Yankee-hater when they left." His throat muscles began tightening, and his voice started breaking. He paused and cleared his throat before continuing. "You see, after they were done with whatever they were doing here, they ransacked the house, and took everything of value—including the emerald. Every generation of the Greene family since then has been attempting to get it back."

"What happened to it?"

"All we know is that it turned up after the war in the private collection of a New York jeweler."

"How did they discover that?"

"In 1871, an article about gem collections in New York City appeared in a magazine. One of the features was about an emerald necklace. There was a drawing. It was the Greene necklace. My great-grandfather literally mortgaged the house so he could finance a trip to New York. When he got there the jeweler denied the truth of the article. My great-grandfather then went to the reporter who wrote the story. The reporter told him that the jeweler said the necklace was purchased from a General. On the way back to the jeweler's shop, my ancestor supposedly fell into the river and drowned. Eliza got a letter a few days later. It was from her husband, my great-grandfather. He apparently wrote it just before he went to see the jeweler the second time."

He reached for his cup of tea, and took a sip. If I didn't know better, I would swear that he had actually lived through the incident he was describing.

"What happened to your great-grandmother?"

"It's a good and bad story there," he said. "My great-grandmother vowed to never leave this house alive. She thought they were going to foreclose on it. When the banker came to see her, he found her dead, in bed. There was a note that said her place would always be in this house. What she did not know was that the bank had forgiven the loan. The banker left the promissory note. 'Satisfied in Full' was written across the top of the document. Her son—my grandfather—moved in, so a

Greene has always lived in this house."

"And she leaves flowers from time to time."

"That's right," he said.

"And the emerald?"

"It will be back in this house where it belongs sooner or later. Every generation in our family knows about the emerald. We keep seeking. One day it will return."

Chapter 9

On Wednesday, all eyes and ears in Canton were on the weather forecast. According to the report on WMGO Radio, there was a 50 percent chance of rain on Thursday, the day of the Canton Flea Market.

Meteorologists were watching a cold front in the Midwest that appeared to be picking up speed. As the front moved south and east, it was expected to encounter warm, moist air moving up from the Gulf of Mexico. Squalls would be breaking out in advance of the front. There was no question as to whether the front would move through central Mississippi. It was only a question of when. If the cold front stayed on its current track, it would not reach Canton until midday on Friday. If its speed increased, it could arrive as early as Thursday morning.

Stormy weather would be of serious concern to all involved with the Flea Market. Customers would not know whether to stay away or go shopping, vendors would have to deal with cloth and canvas booths that were subject to damage by strong winds, and organizers would sadden at the economic impact that a lost day of shopping would bring. There were contingency plans, of course, but a major storm on the day of the event would cause havoc.

I arrived at the Square in Canton in the early after-noon. Activity was in high gear, as vendors prepared for the long setup period. Many would opine that there was never enough time. I went inside Mosby's Gift Shop intending to purchase several Madison County

Courthouse candles as Christmas presents for a few of my friends and relatives. But it is difficult to stop at only a few small items in Mosby's. The antiques and gifts there are alluring. I found an antique jewelry box for my lawyer-girlfriend. It was expensive, but I figured she was worth it. I returned to my car and stashed the gifts in the trunk, then stopped on the north side of the Square for a scoop of ice cream.

My wallet a bit lighter and my stomach a bit fuller, I set out on my quest to find Wanda Watson, wife of Larry Watson and purveyor of clocks. According to the exhibitor guide from the Convention and Visitors Bureau, the Watson Clocks booth would be located on East Fulton Street across from the Old Jail Museum.

Three blocks later, I was standing directly in front of the old jail, a red brick building that is now the home of the Madison County Historical Society. Out of curiosity, I went inside and learned that the jail was completed

in 1870 and was used by the county in that capacity for more than ninety years. The building was also the home of the jailer and his family, who lived upstairs. It was restored by the Madison County Historical Society, and placed on the National Register of Historic Places in 1979. The old cell blocks were restored to their original condition. One of the last escapes from the jail was by a prisoner who had been extradited from Illinois. He found a way to loosen the aged mortar from the bricks with his toothbrush, and headed north toward Chicago.

The Watson Clocks booth was about twelve feet by ten feet. An identifying sign hung on the back canvas wall. Lying on the ground inside the booth were several cardboard boxes, each large enough to hold a half dozen bread boxes. My hunch was that Wanda Watson was parked close by. I walked south, and strolled past an oak-draped cemetery on my right. Sure enough, halfway down the block was a green Chevy Suburban with Florida license plates. On the driver's door was a white magnetic sign with red print identifying the vehicle as belonging to Watson Clocks, Destin, Florida. There was no sign of Wanda Watson, though. Perhaps she was inside the Suburban. Its heavily-tinted side and rear windows prevented a look-see. I did not have to wonder very long. Thirty seconds later, a middle-aged woman holding a Penn's chicken-on-a-stick in her left hand walked up and confronted me.

"Is there something I can do for you?" she asked.

She had a good tan—the kind one would expect from someone who lives in Florida. It went well with her sun-bleached, blond hair. She wore jeans and a Canton

Flea Market tee shirt. Thick black sunglasses hid her eyes. A lady's Rolex hung on her right wrist. I deduced that she must be left-handed. On her feet she wore sandals. Her toenails were painted orange. She had the air of a woman who owned her own business.

"You must be Wanda?" I asked, without any reply from her. "My name is Jack Boulder. I represent the insurance company that has a life insurance policy on your husband. If this is a bad time, I can get in touch with you later."

"It's as good a time as any," she said confidently. "We can talk while I eat lunch, then you can help me unload those boxes inside the truck."

She was not exactly the grieving widow I had mentally prepared for. Direct questions seemed appropriate.

"Are you aware of the accident?"

"Oh, yes," she replied. "The Chief of Police came by and told me about it." She pointed her chicken-on-a-stick at me. "You want a bite?"

"No, thanks," I said. "You don't seem too upset."

"Should I be?"

"Most people are when they lose a spouse," I pointed out.

"Most people aren't married to Larry Watson."

"Was he a bad husband?"

"Look, mister—who are you?"

"I'm a private investigator."

"Well, investigate this," she said taking off her sunglasses to reveal a bruised eye with shades of yellow, black and purple.

"Why did he do that?"

"Said I messed in his business too much."

"When did that happen?"

"Monday night."

"Why didn't you travel together to the Flea Market?"

"I don't know, really. He said that he had some sort of business appointment on Tuesday. When I pressed him about it, he got really angry," she remarked, as she took her last bite of chicken. "He just said he had to fly up here early. Period. End of story."

"Did you know that you are the beneficiary of his life insurance policy?"

"Well, I would hope so."

"Did you know how much he was insured for?"

"He said something about a couple of hundred thousand a few years ago."

"He took out a new policy recently," I said. "For five million dollars."

The news hit her like a direct blow to the face. For a moment, she stared at the asphalt pavement beneath my feet, transfixed by the thought of her new life without her abusive husband, but with plenty of money to spend. Her mouth slowly opened, and she looked back up at me. I expected her to tell me about how her husband was not such a bad fellow, after all. I was way off base on that score.

"When do I get the money?"

"It could be seven years," I answered.

"What? Why so long?"

"They don't have a body. Unless there is some compelling evidence to the contrary, he is not presumed dead for seven years."

"Surely they will find his body soon," she said. "Those big catfish in the reservoir are not that big and hungry, are they?"

"I wouldn't know about that," I said.

"Seven years," she said with a faraway look. "Five million dollars." She shook her head rapidly back and forth, then suddenly seemed to return to normal. "What the hell. How about helping me unload this stuff? I'll back the truck over to the booth. Meet me over there."

I did as she asked. We unloaded about a dozen boxes, several folding tables, chairs and signs. While unloading, she told me that she and Larry had been married for six years. It was his third marriage; her first. Larry was a wheeler-dealer with a wild streak. She thought that after they got married he would settle down. He did for a while, but was always chasing rainbows, searching for the pot of gold—the big deal. Larry rented an airplane about twice a month and flew to flea markets and trade shows when he needed to get there late, or had to be somewhere early the next day. Over the course of their marriage, they had attempted to sell a variety of products on the trade show/flea market circuit. None of their items was ever a big success. But for some reason, the cuckoo clocks they bought from Korea and assembled in their backyard shop had really caught on, so they specialized in cuckoo clocks. She and Larry both had a touch of wanderlust, and their cuckoo clock business provided enough travel opportunities and income for them to live a decent life. To Larry, however, they were always on the verge of making it big.

I listened, then wished her well and drove home. When I arrived at my condo, the answering machine offered a serving of six messages, most of them routine. The last one came in at four fifty-nine p.m. It was my unidentified friend, the one who kept calling about this case. It was now five fifty-five.

"Hello, Jack Boulder," said the female voice. It was tinged with a touch of mockery. "It's time you and I got to meet each other. If you get this message before six-thirty, I'll be waiting for you at the George Street Grocery. It's across the parking lot from the State Justice Building. I'll be on your left as you walk in. Blue jacket. Yellow shirt."

Chapter 10

Fifteen minutes later, I walked through the swinging saloon doors of the George Street Grocery, an old neighborhood grocery store resurrected as a popular watering hole and eatery in the shadow of the state government complex. She was sitting alone at a table against the wall, just like she said.

She was in her mid-twenties with short, brown hair. She wore a blue blazer, soft yellow blouse and a touch of makeup. She reminded me of a marketing rep for a communications company. In other words, she looked like she sold pagers or cellular telephones. I was as wrong as I could be.

"Jack Boulder?" she said, standing up and giving me a firm handshake. I nodded and she gestured toward the seat across the table from her. There was a green, long-neck bottle of imported beer on the table in front of her. Judging by the moisture on the outside of the bottle, I guessed that it had been sitting there for a while. I took a seat and invited her to go first.

"I didn't intend for us to meet, but time is running out—and you don't seem to be making much progress," she said brusquely.

Just as I was about to tell her what she could do with progress, a waitperson appeared and asked, "Are you ready to order now?"

"Yes," said my newfound acquaintance. "We will both have the special."

The server left, and the young woman across the table addressed me before I could speak. "As I said,

Boulder, we don't have much time."

"We are not going to have any time unless you tell me just who you are, and what your connection with this case is," I said firmly, and meant it. I was tired of playing games with this one.

"Fair enough. Here is my card," she said sliding a business card in my direction. On it was imprinted the gold coat of arms of the State of Mississippi and the name and title, "Catherine Greene, Special Assistant Attorney General."

"Are you working on this case, too?" I asked.

She turned her head toward the wall in frustration, then looked back at me. "Boulder, how dumb can you be? I thought that you of all people, Mississippi's great private eye and former St. Louis homicide detective, would be a little quicker on the uptake than that."

I pushed my chair back from the table. I did not have time to be insulted by some preppie attorney, fresh out of law school in her first job.

"Wait! I'm sorry. Don't leave."

"Just get to the point," I said with annoyance.

In one breath she said, "My name is Catherine Greene, my mother's name is Emerald Greene and I grew up in the Greene Mansion in Canton." She inhaled and in another burst said, "My grandfather is the victim of an extortion plot by Larry Watson of Destin, Florida, and tomorrow at the Canton Flea Market, the deal is going down. And I am not working on this case in my official capacity." She paused a long twenty seconds to let it soak in. "Now can we talk?"

"We can talk," I said.

66

"As you know, Grandfather will do anything to get the emerald back. Last week he received an anonymous letter offering the emerald for two-hundred fifty thousand in cash. I'm afraid Grandfather wants to buy it."

"Do you have a copy of the letter?"

She handed me an envelope with the words "Mr. Greene" hand-printed in block letters on the front of it. Inside was a letter that appeared to have been produced by a computer printer.

When Sherman's troops took the Greene emerald, it was sold to a jeweler in New York, who later sold it to a gem collector in London. It was sold on the black market to John Sandhorn in 1990. It is now available to you for $250,000 firm. If you desire to make this purchase, leave your living room light on all night tomorrow.

"I presume your grandfather left the light on," I said.

"Of course," she replied. "He received a telephone call the next morning, instructing him to have Mother leave a suitcase filled with the cash in the old Trolio Hotel lobby at exactly ten-thirty on the day of the Flea Market. She is to tell the receptionist that a Mr. Beckham will be picking up the suitcase. At ten forty-five, Grandfather is supposed to go to the Watson Clocks booth and purchase the cuckoo clock that has its hands set for four-forty. The emerald will be inside the clock."

"If he is telling the truth," I remarked as our food arrived at the table. "When was the last contact with this guy?"

"Tuesday, a week ago," she said.

"No contact since then?"

"None," she answered.

"And you think it's Larry Watson?"

"Isn't it obvious? An emerald is stolen from a museum owned by a person of questionable integrity the night after my grandfather agrees to pay a quarter million dollars for the family heirloom, which just also happens to be an emerald. The instructions call for picking up the gem in a clock from a Destin vendor, who is Larry Watson, a known con artist." Her voice was rising. "I did my homework, Boulder."

"Why haven't you called in the police or the FBI?"

"There is a chance that this emerald really is the Greene emerald. If it is, then my family is entitled to it. It is stolen property that should be returned to its rightful owner."

"What about the statute of limitations?" I asked.

"That could be an issue, but I have already done some checking. The Greene emerald was taken from its owners in time of war, similar to the Nazi and Russian art thefts of World War II. Lately there has been an international effort to have artwork stolen in wartime returned to the rightful owners. I have been talking to an aide to one of our United States senators from Mississippi who happens to have a strong interest in this subject. He is considering opening the issue of southern artwork taken during the Civil War, to be returned to its rightful owners. Our case is only one of many."

"The Civil War is over, Miss Greene."

"You are correct. But the damage, misery, and suffering that it caused live on. Did you know that in 1863, when the Union Army invaded Canton to destroy the Dixie Ordnance Works and tear up the railroad tracks, they also burned down most of the Square?" Her face was flush and her words were coming out like volleys from an air cannon. "After their ransacking, those damn Yankees sent word back north that there was not a dollar's worth of public property left in Canton. Take a look at the buildings around the Square. The dates on them are mostly after the Civil War. It is such a shame."

She lowered her head and began playing with her food with her fork. She was passionate about this, and she had let too much of that passion be revealed. I would wager that she grew up hearing the Civil War story from her grandfather. Would recovering the emerald bring closure? After a couple of minutes she composed herself.

"I'm sorry," she said. "I didn't mean to get side-tracked by the Civil War. Back to answering your question—if I go to the police the best they can do is arrest Larry Watson and recover some stolen property. Who knows if the emerald in question is even the one from our family. My grandfather would be dead before the legal issues got resolved. If we get the emerald now, and the police get Larry Watson, then I will be in a much better position to regain our rightful ownership of the emerald."

"In other words, possession is nine-tenths of ownership," I said.

"Something like that," she replied.

"One other minor question."

"What's that?" she replied.

"What if Larry Watson is dead?"

"Then your client gets to pay out a lot of money."

Chapter 11

Before we left the restaurant, we devised a plan. Tomorrow, Catherine Greene would stake out the Watson Clocks booth, while I kept watch over the Trolio Hotel. We would stay in touch by cellular telephone. I was to call her when the drop was made, and when the suitcase was picked up. She would call me when her grandfather bought the clock. The way we had it figured, her mother would drop off the suitcase at ten-thirty, the suitcase would be picked up by a third party or Larry Watson himself before ten forty-five and then her grandfather would pick up the clock at ten forty-five. We would stay in touch, but play it by ear.

After we finished our meal and concocted our plan, I went back to my condominium. The night air was humid. It was hotter than normal for this time of year. I thought I smelled rain in the air. I kicked off my walking shoes, propped my feet on the coffee table, and began to mentally review the facts that I had so far. I told myself to remember who my client was. My job was to find out if Larry Watson was alive. This other stuff was interesting, but ancillary. That was easy to say, but hard to remove from my mind.

First, there was the obvious question: Why would Larry Watson fake his death? Surely he must have known that the insurance company would not automatically pay off. Who would benefit if they did? His wife was the beneficiary, and she did not even know it. At least she did not know the amount of the policy. I found that to be strange. Earlier in my life, I had been married for a short time. When I took out an insurance policy and named my wife as beneficiary, I couldn't wait to tell her about it. It's a natural thing to tell your wife. I recalled the joke about being worth more dead than alive. In that case, the spouse would have a motive. Indeed, the beneficiary is always the first suspect in an unusual death. But Wanda Watson said she didn't know anything about the policy. If that were true, then she would have no motive. Besides, how would she have done it—sabotage the plane? It seemed highly unlikely, but not altogether impossible.

Perhaps Larry and Wanda had hatched up a plot to extort a quarter million dollars from old Mr. Greene. They have probably been exhibiting at the Canton Flea Market for years. That would have given them an opportunity to meet him. If they somehow knew of his yearning to recover the emerald, they may have plotted the extortion when an emerald of significant size and value was exhibited at the Sandhorn Museum. If such were the case, then why would Larry fake his death? That did not make much sense.

What if it were true that Larry Watson had died in the plane crash and the body really was missing? If the Watsons were pulling a scam, then who would pick up the suitcase? I made a mental note to ask Catherine during our stakeout if Wanda Watson was in the booth. If she left at ten-twenty, it would suggest that Larry may really be missing.

There was the possibility that it was someone else— someone not even connected with the Watsons. For some reason, my first thought was Catherine Greene.

What if she was scamming her own grandfather? Maybe she and her mother were in on it together. Family members are always good suspects. Besides, Catherine seemed to know a lot about things, even if she did have access to classified information through her position. Nevertheless, I sensed that there was more here. I decided it was best not to trust Catherine yet.

I made a few notes on things to do before going to Canton tomorrow morning. The Chief of Law Enforcement at the Barnett Reservoir should be contacted to make certain that a body had not been found. I would call my client and give him an update. I also needed to remind myself to get up early, so as not to forget my daily two-mile jog.

By the time the ten o'clock news came on television, I had made a lengthy list of things to do. I settled back and watched with mild interest. There was a "Good News" segment on one station that featured the Canton Flea Market. It told of how thousands of shoppers would be there, but that the chance of rain was increasing. The cold front had picked up speed, and was now over northern Missouri, Illinois and Kansas. If it continued its present march and rate, it would be here by mid-afternoon tomorrow. "So take your umbrellas to Canton, just in case," preached the meteorologist.

Before retiring for bed, I picked up the file I had made on this case. I reviewed Larry Watson's application one more time. I was just about to put it back down, when I saw it. There was an alternate beneficiary listed on the application. It was none other than Emerald Greene, artist.

Chapter 12

The noise from the telephone interrupted my slumber. It was difficult to wake up. I'd had trouble getting the case out of my mind earlier, and sleep would not come. Now that it had arrived, I was deep in the rapid eye movement phase where sleep is the soundest. Finally I picked up the telephone receiver with my right hand, and looked over at the digital display on the clock beside my bed. The red numbers told me it was one fourteen a.m. This call had better be good.

"Hello," I groaned.

"Mr. Boulder," said a female voice, which I didn't recognize. "I know it's late, but I must see you right away. Meet me as soon as possible at the truck stop restaurant where Highway 22 meets the interstate. It's a matter of life and death."

"Who's death?"

"Mine."

"Who is this?"

"Wanda."

"Wanda who?" I was beginning to wake up.

"Wanda Watson," she said intensely. "They are going to try to kill me."

"Who is going to try to kill you?"

"Just please hurry. That's all."

It was a struggle, but five minutes later I was awake and getting dressed. I brushed my teeth, and as I was doing so, wondered why I had thought to do that. I retrieved my car and headed north. The night was still and humid. Twenty minutes later, I was exiting Interstate

55 to a glut of all-night convenience stores, gasoline stations, and chain fast food restaurants. Only one of the restaurants appeared to be locally owned. As I pulled into its parking lot, I immediately noticed the Suburban with Florida plates. Inside a large plate glass window, I saw Wanda Watson hunched over a table with both hands wrapped around a cup of coffee. She looked up in anticipation as my headlights hit the window. When I walked in, she looked me straight in the eye, but did not move. I took a seat across from her and ordered coffee. She didn't have her sunglasses on, so her black eye was more noticeable. Here, under fluorescent lights, it looked horrible. He must have really smacked her.

"What's up, Ms. Watson?" I said calmly, with just a touch of irritation. I wanted her to know that this better be important.

"I lied to you earlier," she said to her cup of coffee.

"How's that?"

"Larry's not dead. I saw him an hour ago," she said, still keeping her head down.

"Would you care to start from the beginning?" I said as my java arrived.

She took a sip and began, still holding onto the coffee cup with both hands. "Larry had a plan. Somehow, he found out about this emerald that had been stolen from a family in Canton. He also knew that the old man would pay a fortune to get it back. So he cooked up this plan to steal an emerald from a museum in Destin, and sell it to the old man for a lot of money—a quarter of a million dollars. I didn't think the old man had that much money, but apparently he does."

With trembling hands and a clinking sound, she set the cup back in the saucer. She needed to keep talking. She finally looked me in the eye.

"Go on," I encouraged.

"The plan was very simple. The old man was to bring a suitcase full of cash to our booth, and we would give him a clock with the emerald inside it. I didn't see how there was much to go wrong."

"So, what went wrong?"

"Larry said he needed to fly to Jackson early, to take care of some other business. When I asked him what business he was talking about, he became very irritated. I raised my voice; he raised his voice. We got into an argument, then he slugged me. All I wanted to know was why it was so necessary to rent a plane to go to Jackson and back."

"Tell me about the burglary at the museum," I said.

"Somehow, Larry found out that the emerald was at the museum. I don't know how. He likes to buy and sell antiques, but he never goes to museums. He doesn't have a whole lot of culture. Anyway, he said that Sandhorn had bought the emerald on the black market, and would not even file a police report. I thought he was going to—you know—shoplift it somehow. I didn't think he would commit a burglary."

"Do you know if he actually did the burglary?"

"I think so. He was gone all night," she said, lowering her head. I knew what that meant.

"Why are you lying to me, Wanda?"

At that question, she started crying. A steady stream of tears, followed by loud sniffles. I handed her a half dozen small napkins from the dispenser on the table. Even though she didn't boo-hoo, the sniffling was loud enough to attract the attention of several truckers sitting nearby. A beefy, pot-bellied man with tousled, greasy black hair under a Peterbilt Trucks baseball hat scooted back from his table and walked menacingly toward our table. On his dark blue uniform shirt was a name tag that read "Bubba." He puffed out his chest and said to Wanda, "This here punk bothering you, ma'am?"

"No. I'm fine, thank you," she replied, as she wiped away the last of the tears from her now red eyes.

He looked threateningly at me and then said to her. "If he gives you any trouble, ma'am, I'll be right over there."

She thanked him, and he walked back to his table. He sipped from a coffee cup, and glued his eyes on us.

Her composure regained, she asked, "Now, where were we?"

"You were about to tell me why you were lying to me about the burglary," I said coldly.

"Okay," she confessed. "I did help with the museum. He went inside and I stayed outside as the lookout, or whatever you call it."

"How did he get in?"

"He had a pair of metal shears. He just cut through the wall. He came out with a bag of stuff and we went back home."

"When did you first see the emerald?"

"When we got home," she said. "He took it out of the bag and showed it to me. He said this was going to change our lives forever."

Chapter 13

The waitress appeared and refilled our coffee cups. Bubba the Truck Driver realized that he was not going to rescue this damsel in distress, so he paid his tab and went back to his big rig. As it pulled out onto Highway 22, I resumed the conversation.

"So who's going to kill you?"

"Larry—and that woman."

"What woman?"

"That Greene woman. I think her name is Emerald Greene."

"Go slowly and give me the details."

"This evening, I couldn't sleep, so I decided to go walking. Even at midnight, there is a lot of activity in the area where the flea market booths are set up. I walked over a few blocks and came across a big house with the lights on downstairs. I looked in the window —and there was Larry! I wasn't sure, at first. After all, he was supposed to be dead. So I tiptoed up to the window to make sure that it was him."

She was becoming more animated now. As she told the story, she was mentally walking through it all over again. I saw no need to interrupt.

"Just as I got to this big azalea bush in front of the window, he walked out of the room to the back of the house," she continued, her words coming a little faster. "I went around to the backyard and hid in the bushes. I had a good view into a room that had lots of windows. There were paintings inside. After a few minutes, a woman came into the room. She walked over and put her arms around Larry's neck and kissed him." She was becoming flush with anger. "She kissed my husband!"

"And what did you do at that point?" I asked.

"I almost jumped out of those bushes and went right inside, screaming. If I had had a gun, I would have killed them both, right there. But I kept my cool. I stayed in the flower bushes."

"What happened next?" I prodded.

"After they finished kissing, they came out of the back door, sat down at an outdoor table and started talking. I thought I was going to pass out, holding my breath so they wouldn't hear me. I was only that far away from them," she said motioning to the table where Bubba had been sitting. "He told her that everything was going as planned and at this time tomorrow, they would be on an island somewhere. That rat!"

"What else did he say?" I asked, wincing at the spittle she had sent to my face.

"I'm getting to that. Just hold on," she said wiping her lips with a napkin then wiping my cheek. "Sorry about that. Anyway, she asked him when he was going to 'do the deed.' Of course, I thought she meant getting the emerald. He said that it would be taken care of right after the emerald was in his hands. Then he said that he was going to rig the Suburban to explode when the back door was opened. That's when I realized that he was planning to kill me!"

"What else did he say about that?"

"That was all," she said. "Then she started talking about how her daddy was going to be happy to have the emerald back, and how happy she was going to be to finally have a life of her own. Everybody was going to be so happy."

"Except you."

"Yeah, except me," she said. "I'll be dead. What am I going to do?"

That was a good question, and one that I was not prepared to answer. If she went to the police, she would likely be held for accessory to burglary. I was certainly not going to take her in. There was only one thing to do, and that would be to play this thing out.

"Where's the emerald now?"

"I guess Larry has it. He took it with him when he took off in the plane."

"Ms. Watson, I'm going to tell it like it is," I said. "You don't need me. You need a lawyer. You've assisted with a burglary. You have . . ."

"My life is in danger," she broke in before I could finish the sentence. "I need a bodyguard. Don't private investigators do that kind of work?"

"Not this one," I said.

"Well, I guess I called the wrong number, didn't I?" she said, and got up and walked out with a haughty step.

I paid the ticket and went back home to a short night of fitful sleep.

Chapter 14

Catherine Greene and I met at eight o'clock Thursday morning at the rest stop on Interstate 55, just south of Canton. Surrounded by motor noise from a dozen eighteen-wheel tractor-trailers, we stood outside our little cars and began strategizing. The smell of diesel exhaust and the humid air made for a low comfort level. Overhead, the clouds were beginning to build, and the wind was picking up.

She was dressed in blue jeans, cowboy boots, and a denim shirt with a logo stitched in orange that read "Mississippi Hot Air Balloon Championship." She was driving a red Miata with the top down. I was wearing my usual khaki slacks and a "Canton Pilgrimage" polo shirt that the lady at the Chamber of Commerce had given me. I was driving my Camaro; the windows were rolled down.

Last night I made the decision not to tell Catherine that her mother was the alternate beneficiary on Larry Watson's life insurance policy. Speculation about such a situation could only lead to conclusions that were not honorable. I also withheld the information about her mother and Larry Watson.

We reviewed our plan from last night, and decided that not much needed changing. If Larry Watson came into the old Trolio Hotel and picked up the suitcase, then I would call Catherine, and she would immediately call the police while I followed Watson. The first confrontation with Watson would be by the police. If someone else picked up the suitcase, I would follow them until the suitcase was turned over to someone else. If the subject got into a vehicle and departed, then I would attempt to follow. If, in my judgment, I could not follow, then I would call Catherine, who would call in the police. She suggested we park our cars one block north of the Square for easier access. She would call me when the cuckoo clock set at four-forty was purchased by her grandfather. She would also discreetly follow her grandfather, in case anyone had stealing the clock from him as part of the plan.

"Won't your grandfather recognize you?" I asked.

"I'm good at tailing people," she said. "Besides, he won't recognize me.

The plan, such as it was, was okay. But I didn't like it. I felt like I was being swept up in a series of events over which I had no control. Besides, this was not my fight. I had been hired to determine if Larry Watson was alive or dead. I now had an eyewitness to the fact that he was alive. It would have been just fine with me to let the local police or FBI handle this. But I understood. I knew that they would want to corroborate information before committing to a plan of action. There was no time to call the Feds, and the locals had all they could handle with the thousands of people about to converge on Canton.

So I would ride it out and hope for the best. Most of the time there are identifiable good guys and bad guys in cases like this. Someone to associate with, some good cause. It seemed that everybody in this case was dirty. Even old grandpa was willing to pay a ransom for stolen property.

We went north—she first, and me following in my Camaro, on the interstate to the North Canton exit, then south on Highway 51 just north of the Square. Already, parking spaces in private lots and yards were being sold for ten dollars apiece. Adjacent to the Square, spots would sell for twenty-five dollars. We got lucky and found two spaces on the street, one block north of the Square. She emerged from her Miata, sporting dark sunglasses and a cowboy hat. We verified that we each had our cellular phones. Then she went her way, and I went mine. In less than an hour and half, whatever was going to happen would unfold.

I headed toward the Square, an aroma of cooking odors already finding its way to my nostrils. As I walked onto the Square, I surveyed the sight in front of me. Tents and booths were lined up next to each other on both sides of the street. The middle lane of the street was left as a walking space. Already, someone was pur-

chasing a cajun steak-ka-bob. It was not even ten o'clock a.m. The first booth I encountered was adorned with all types of items made of snakeskin. There were snakeskin wallets, snakeskin belts, snakeskin boots and snakeskin purses. There was even a snakeskin necktie. There were also all different kinds of snakeskins. Moccasin and rattlers appeared to be the most popular. Another booth had an assortment of herbal soaps.

A long line had already formed at the weather vane booth beside the courthouse. It was easy to see why. For an excellent price, purchasers could get a weather vane with a choice of adornments on the top. There were hogs, geese, roosters, farmers on tractors, and boys catching fish.

In front of the Trolio Hotel, home of the Convention and Visitors Bureau, there were booths lined up wall-to-wall, leaving only the canopied sidewalk. It would be easy to hide myself in the crowd, but I would need to be alert to make certain that I saw anyone going inside with a suitcase. I now had forty-five minutes until the designated time. I strolled around and took in the sights, sounds, and smells of what seemed like a fair rather than a flea market. What surprised me most was the intensity of some of the shoppers. It was as if they knew what they wanted, and had to be the first to get it. I wondered if any of the vendors ever ran out of merchandise. Around the Square, there were booths featuring baskets, calligraphy, pottery, Christmas orna-ments, dolls, jewelry, metalwork and much more. This was indeed a Christmas shopper's heaven. By ten-fif-teen I had almost forgotten the reason I was here. I'm not the shopping sort, but this was worthwhile because of its uniqueness and variety.

I stationed myself fifteen feet from the front door of the old hotel and pretended to be shopping at a booth featuring woodcarvings. The door was busy with people going in and out. Then I saw a suitcase being carried down the sidewalk toward the front door. It was old, blue, and large, and strapped onto a luggage carrier with wheels. I guess a quarter of a million dollars weighs a few pounds. As expected, Emerald Greene was pulling the carrier. She looked out of place in her plaid skirt, red long-sleeve blouse and penny loafers. She wore a silk scarf around her neck, a black beret and wire-rimmed sunglasses. She looked like a traveler.

She went inside the front door. I moved quickly toward it, and attempted to enter. I wanted to hear what she said to the person inside. But, as I pulled open the door, a group of six women filed out of the door, thanking me for holding it for them. The seventh person in the line was Emerald Greene. She stared straight ahead, and apparently did not recognize me. I went inside the lobby, and was greeted by a receptionist behind a desk. There was a door to a larger room at the rear. I saw a stack of brochures on a counter, and asked if I could pick one up. She smiled and invited me to take my time. I planned on doing exactly that. The brochures were about Canton sights, and the Allison's Wells School of Arts and Crafts. As I was glancing at the latter, I heard a male voice say, "Do you have a suitcase for Mr. Beckham?"

"Yes sir. It's right here," said the receptionist.

Chapter 15

Larry Watson grasped the handle on the carrier and pulled the suitcase behind him. He went out the front door, and I fell in fifteen feet behind him. He was wearing a blue blazer, light blue dress shirt, gray slacks and a silly-looking tan golf cap. He, too, wore dark sunglasses. He negotiated the crowd and headed east on Center Street. I paused at a puppet demonstration, pulled out my cell phone, and dialed Catherine Greene's number. She answered on the first ring.

"I'm following Watson on Center Street on the north side of the Square. Go ahead and send the police this way," I said softly and firmly into the device.

"Will do," came her reply. "Will call back and confirm."

Watson continued east on Center Street, zigging and zagging back and forth to avoid the sea of people arriving in Canton. When he got to the Greene Mansion, he turned up in the driveway. As he walked briskly towards the house, my cell phone let loose with its electronic warble. I answered immediately.

"Where do you need the police?" she asked.

"Send them to the Greene Mansion," I said, followed by a long five seconds of dead air.

"I'll take care of it," she said and hung up.

I walked past the large house, then stopped and peered around a bush. It was a good thirty yards from the street to the front door. I stepped out and went along the length of the neighbor's yard, concealed from the Greene Mansion by a hedgerow. Finally, I inched along until I was beside the house. In the backyard, I saw a car with its trunk open. The police had better hurry. A trip was about to be taken. I inched closer to the rear corner of the house and peered around it. I came face-to-face with Larry Watson, holding a .38 caliber Chief's Special in his right hand. It was pointed right between my eyes.

"Looking for someone?" he asked.

I had to think of something fast. The best I could do was, "Is this the Hospitality House for the artists' reception?"

"Of course, it is. Won't you please come in?" He kept the gun to my head as we went through the back door to Emerald Greene's studio. As we entered, Emerald Greene came through the door from the living room. She quickly analyzed the sight of me standing in the middle of her studio, with her boyfriend holding a gun on me.

"Is this someone you know?" Watson said to her.

"Yes, he was here the other night asking lots of questions about ghosts and such."

"What do you want to do with him?" asked Watson.

From that question I made an instant deduction—Emerald Greene was behind this caper. She was the one in charge. He was asking her what to do. I needed to buy some time. Hopefully, the police would arrive any minute. I took a chance and started walking to the living room. I wanted to be seen from the street.

Turning to Emerald Greene, I said, "Looks like the emerald is finally coming home to roost. I guess the ghost of your great-great-grandmother will be very happy." I was now in the living room and both of them were coming over the threshold. "Tell me, Emerald. Do you think he got the real Greene emerald?"

"Shut up," she yelled, then turned to Watson. "Take him upstairs, put something over that gun to muffle the noise, and shoot him. Then put him in the closet at the top of the stairs. Daddy never checks it, and we will be long gone before he starts stinking. We've got to get out of here. There is a plane to catch—in case you have forgotten. I'll be waiting for you in the car."

Watson pointed the pistol at me and said, "You heard her. Move it."

I raised my hands above my head, and just stood there. With all the people walking by in front of the house, surely someone would look in and see what was going on. I could tell Watson was getting anxious.

"You heard me. Get going," he said.

"No, I don't think so, Larry. If you are going to kill me, I prefer that you do it here. Why should I make it easy for by walking up the stairs? Besides, who knows who might see you here. It would wrap up the case rather nicely."

"Nobody even knows I'm alive," he said.

"That's where you are dead wrong," I said. "Don't you remember last night? Your wife remembers seeing you alive."

He was a desperate man now. His plan was coming unraveled. Unfortunately, I wasn't leaving him very many options. He would have to shoot me to have any chance of getting away with his plan.

Just then, a Canton police car pulled into the driveway and drove up to the side of the house. There was a passenger in the front seat who looked a lot like Catherine. Watson bolted out the door to the backyard. I followed right behind. He ran for the driver's door of the car in which Emerald Greene was calmly sitting. I heard a loud, "Freeze, or I'll shoot," and saw that the police officer had his gun drawn on Watson. Emerald Greene screamed, "Shoot him."

But Larry Watson knew when the odds were stacked against him. He lowered his gun and dropped it to the ground. The police officer radioed for backup, and was told that it may be a few minutes because other officers were so busy. The officer then herded us all into the living room. He handcuffed Larry Watson and Emerald Greene to each other's wrist, and made them get down on their knees. Catherine and I took a seat on the sofa, and the officer remained standing. It was an interesting collection of people.

Before anyone could speak, the front door opened, and in walked George Greene. He was carrying a dark brown cuckoo clock.

Chapter 16

George Greene surveyed the scene before him, then looked at the police officer for an explanation. I decided to speak up.

"Welcome home, Mr. Greene," I said. "We were just in the process of recovering your money and arresting the people who attempted to extort it from you."

"What?" he asked in a state of dismay and confusion.

"Just a moment, I'll be right back," I said. I walked outside to the car and retrieved the suitcase. Returning to the living room, I set it in the middle of the floor. "Does this look familiar, Mr. Greene?"

He just stood there, not saying a thing. I attempted to open the suitcase, but it was locked.

"Catherine, would you search your mother for the key?"

As she started toward her mother, Emerald Greene said, "It's in my skirt pocket."

Catherine removed the key and opened the briefcase. It was full of hundred dollar bills, most of which looked used. The police officer now looked the most confused. I looked at him and he said, "Would you care to enlighten me?"

"I believe I can now do that," I said. "You see that emerald in the painting up there over the mantle?" All eyes focused on the matriarch with the emerald necklace. "According to Mr. Greene that emerald was stolen from this house over a hundred years ago. Every generation of the family has vowed to get it back. Emerald here saw a way to cash in." I looked directly at the artist.

"Emerald had her art displayed in Destin, Florida, home of Mr. Larry Watson here. I would have to guess on this point, but . . . Emerald, did you and Larry meet when he was here for the flea market, or did you meet when you went to Destin?"

"Go to blazes," she blurted.

"It really doesn't matter," I continued. "What matters is that they apparently fell in love and wanted to spend the rest of their lives together. Unfortunately, Larry here is not only already married, but he scrapes by from month to month. All they needed was money. Emerald told the family story about the emerald to Larry, then it was discovered that there was an emerald on display at the Sandhorn Museum. My guess is that Emerald probably went to a museum function while in Destin. Larry is not known as an art lover—are you, Larry?"

Larry did not say a word. He just stayed bowed on his knees handcuffed to his girlfriend.

"All they had to do now was send a note to Mr. Greene and ask for money. But they knew Mr. Greene would not respond to just any note. That's why they gave details known by Mr. Greene. It was a way to validate that the emerald—the one that is presumably in the cuckoo clock that Mr. Greene is holding—was in fact the family jewel."

Everyone turned to Mr. Greene, who stood there awkwardly holding the cuckoo clock. He looked down at it, then tossed it over to a large chair. It bounced on the seat cushion then hit the floor, cuckooing once as it did so.

"I'm afraid I have really been the fool," said Mr. Greene. "There was no emerald."

"Where is it, Watson?" I demanded.

"Try the bottom of your reservoir," he said with a sneer.

Addressing the group I said, "Watson really thought he could get away with this, but there was one thing he didn't know—without a body there is no payoff for seven years. He listed his wife on a five million dollar policy as the beneficiary, and included an alternate beneficiary—Emerald Greene. She would receive the money if Wanda Watson died and had no heirs or a will. Which brings me to the Canton Police Department's immediate challenge."

"What's that?" said the officer.

"Last night Watson's wife overheard him and Emerald discussing a bomb for Ms. Watson's vehicle. It's a Chevy Suburban with Florida plates parked beside the cemetery behind the Old Jail Museum. Your people may find that there is a bomb rigged to go off when the back door is opened."

Just then, a marked Canton police cruiser and the unmarked car of the police chief pulled into the driveway. The first officer on the scene led Watson and Emerald Greene away. As he did so, I heard him dispatching another officer to the Watson Clocks booth to make certain that Ms. Watson did not open the door of her vehicle. The Chief said that he would take the suitcase of money, to which Catherine responded that she wanted it counted in front of two witnesses and a receipt from the Chief before it could leave the house.

There were the usual formalities to be taken care of. I promised to give a statement to the District Attorney's investigator tomorrow. There were still a few loose ends for the police to tie up, but they had a good case against Larry Watson and Emerald Greene. I didn't know what would happen to Wanda Watson, but it was not my place to become involved in her life. There were no explosions at the Canton Flea Market, so she must have fared well. I hoped that she sold a lot of cuckoo clocks. I couldn't help feeling for George Greene. Who knows? The emerald may have really been the Greene emerald.

I spent the remainder of the afternoon browsing, eating, and shopping at the flea market. I looked at the brochure in my pocket about Christmas in Canton. I would return. Christmas in Canton at the Priestly House had a nice ring to it.

EPILOGUE

The following morning, George Greene and his granddaughter, Catherine, sat in the living room of the Greene Mansion sipping coffee and gazing up at the fresh flowers on the mantle.

"She came back last night," said the old man pensively. "The flowers are especially nice."

Catherine reached over to the coffee table, picked up an item and walked over to the painting of her ancestor. She held up a sixty-carat emerald and compared it to the one in the painting.

"This is it, Granddaddy," she said decisively. "No doubt about it."

"You're a genius Catherine. You have made an old man proud. I didn't think we could pull it off."

"We almost didn't make it," she said. "I had to give Jack Boulder a lot of help. But he came through for us."

"Yes. The flowers are nice today."